Cool Duck
&
Lots of Hats

Early ★ Reader

First American edition published in 2019 by Lerner Publishing Group, Inc.

An original concept by Elizabeth Dale
Copyright © 2019 Elizabeth Dale

Illustrated by Giusi Capizzi

First published by Maverick Arts Publishing Limited

Maverick
arts publishing

Licensed Edition
Cool Duck & Lots of Hats

Lerner Publications Company
A division of Lerner Publishing Group, Inc.
241 First Avenue North
Minneapolis, MN 55401 USA

For reading levels and more information, look up this title at
www.lernerbooks.com.

Main body text set in Mikado a. Typeface provided by HVD Fonts.

Library of Congress Cataloging-in-Publication Data
Names: Dale, Elizabeth, 1952– author. | Capizzi, Giusy, illustrator. | Dale,
    Elizabeth, 1952– Cool duck. | Dale, Elizabeth, 1952– Lots of hats.
Title: Cool duck ; and Lots of hats / by Elizabeth Dale ; illustrated by Giusi
    Capizzi.
Description: First American edition, licensed edition. | Minneapolis : Lerner
    Publications, 2019. | Series: Early bird readers. Pink (Early bird stories).
Identifiers: LCCN 2018017783 (print) | LCCN 2018026028 (ebook) |
    ISBN 9781541543232 (eb pdf) | ISBN 9781541541573 (lb : alk. paper) |
    ISBN 9781541546202 (pb : alk. paper)
Subjects: LCSH: Readers—Animals. | Readers—Hats. | Readers (Primary) |
    Animals—Juvenile literature. | Hats—Juvenile literature.
Classification: LCC PE1127.A6 (ebook) | LCC PE1127.A6 D225 2019 (print) |
    DDC 428.6/2—dc23

LC record available at https://lccn.loc.gov/2018017783

Manufactured in the United States of America
1-45331-38981-5/30/2018

EARLY BIRD STORIES

Cool Duck
&
Lots of Hats

Elizabeth Dale

Illustrated by
Giusi Capizzi

Lerner Publications ◆ Minneapolis

The Letter "D"

Trace the lowercase and uppercase letter with a finger. Sound out the letter.

Around,

up,

down

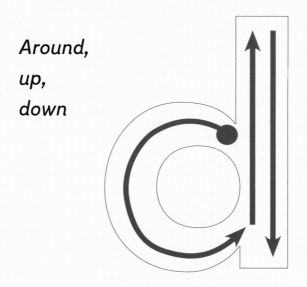

Down,

up,

around

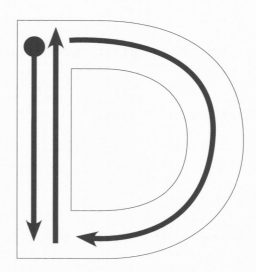

Some words to familiarize:

hot   splash   duck

High-frequency words:

the is

Tips for Reading *Cool Duck*

- *Practice the words listed above before reading the story.*

- *If the reader struggles with any of the other words, ask them to look for sounds they know in the word. Encourage them to sound out the words and help them read the words if necessary.*

- *After reading the story, ask the reader why Cat and Dog are not hot or fed up at the end of the story.*

Fun Activity

Discuss all the different things you can do to keep cool.

Cool Duck

The cat is hot.

The duck is cool.

The dog is hot.

Splash!

The dog is cool.

The cat is cool.

The duck is cool!

The Letter "H"

Trace the lowercase and uppercase letter with a finger. Sound out the letter.

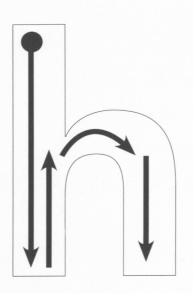

*Down,
up,
around,
down*

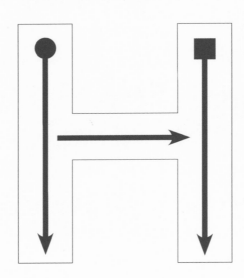

*Down,
lift
down,
across*

Some words to familiarize:

dog   hat   big

High-frequency words:

has of a the

Tips for Reading *Lots of Hats*

- Practice the tricky words listed above before reading the story.

- If the reader struggles with any of the other words, ask them to look for sounds they know in the word. Encourage them to sound out the words and help them read the words if necessary.

- After reading the story, ask the reader why the dog ends up with all the hats.

Fun Activity

How many types of hat can you think of?

When do you wear each one?

Lots of Hats

Sam has a big hat.

Come back, hat.

Dad has a big, **big** hat.

Mom has a big, **big**, **big** hat.

The dog has lots of hats!

Leveled for Guided Reading

Early Bird Stories have been edited and leveled by leading educational consultants to correspond with guided reading levels. The levels are assigned by taking into account the content, language style, layout, and phonics used in each book.

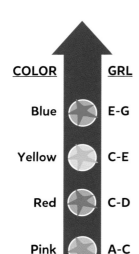

COLOR		GRL
Blue		E-G
Yellow		C-E
Red		C-D
Pink		A-C